Natasha and the Letter N

Alphabet Friends

by Cynthia Klingel and Robert B. Noyed

The Child's World®

Note to parents and educators:

The first skill children acquire before becoming successful readers is individual letter recognition. The Alphabet Friends series has been created with the needs of young learners in mind. Each engaging book begins by showing the difference between the capital letter and the lowercase letter. In each of the books on the vowels and the consonants c and g, children are introduced to the different sounds that the letter can make. Finally, children see that the letters can be found at the beginning of a word, in the middle of a word, and in most cases, at the end of a word.

Following the introduction, children meet their Alphabet Friends. The friend in each story encounters many words that include the featured letter of that book.

Each noun that begins with the title letter is highlighted in red with the initial letter of the word in bold. Above the word is a rebus drawing that establishes a strong picture cue.

At the end of each book, we have included three words lists. Can your young learners find all the words in each book with the title letter in them?

Published in the United States of America by The Child's World®
P.O. Box 326
Chanhassen, MN 55317-0326
800-599-READ
www.childsworld.com

The Child's World®, Mary Berendes, Publishing Director

Editorial Directions, Inc.: E. Russell Primm, Editorial Director; Emily Dolbear, Line Editor; Ruth Martin, Editorial Assistant; Linda S. Koutris, Photo Researcher and Selector

Photographs ©: Janis Christie/Photodisc/Getty Images: Cover & 9; David Buffington/Photodisc/Getty Images: 10; Image Source/elektraVision/Picture Quest: 13; Corbis/Picture Quest: 14; Ryan McVay/Photodisc/Getty Images: 17; Randy Allbritton/Photodisc/Getty Images: 18; Randy Allbritton/Photodisc/Picture Quest: 21.

Library of Congress Cataloging-in-Publication Data
Klingel, Cynthia Fitterer.
Natasha and the letter N / by Cynthia Klingel and Robert B. Noyed.
p. cm. — (Alphabet readers)
Summary: A simple story about all the things that Natasha needs to do at night introduces the letter "n".
ISBN 1-59296-104-5 (Library Bound : alk. paper)
[1. Night–Fiction. 2. Alphabet.] I. Noyed, Robert B. II. Title. III. Series.
PZ7.K6798Nat 2003
[E]–dc21
2003006603

Let's learn about the letter **N.**

The letter **N** can look like this: **N.**

The letter **N** can also look like this: **n.**

The letter **n** can be at the beginning of a word, like newspaper.

newspaper

The letter **n** can be in the middle of a word, like banana.

ba**n**ana

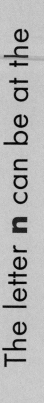

The letter **n** can be at the end of a word, like horn.

hor**n**

Nighttime is busy for **N**atasha. She has

many things she needs to do. It seems

Natasha never has enough time!

Natasha needs to read the **n**ewspaper.

She writes some information in her

notebook for school.

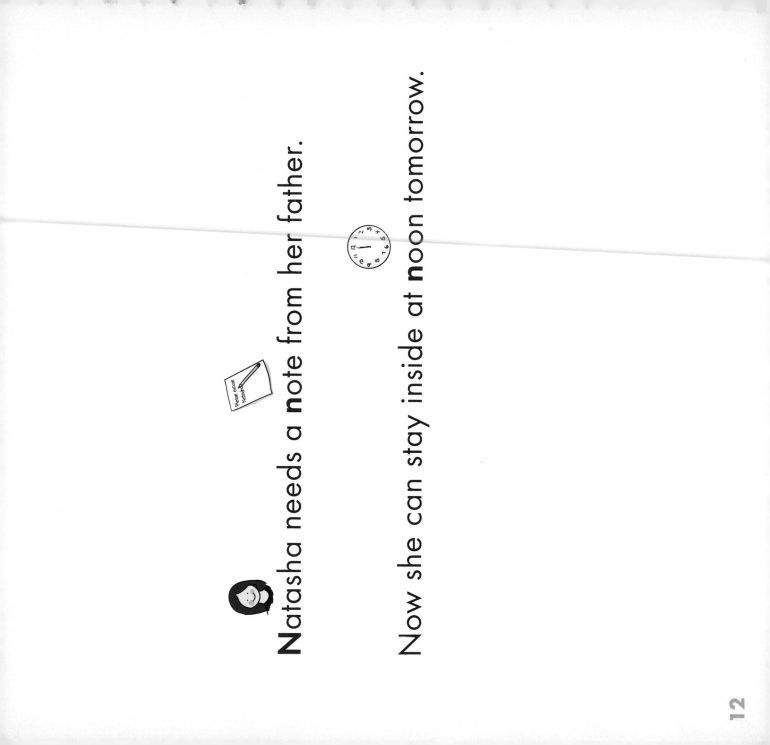

Natasha needs a **n**ote from her father.

Now she can stay inside at **n**oon tomorrow.

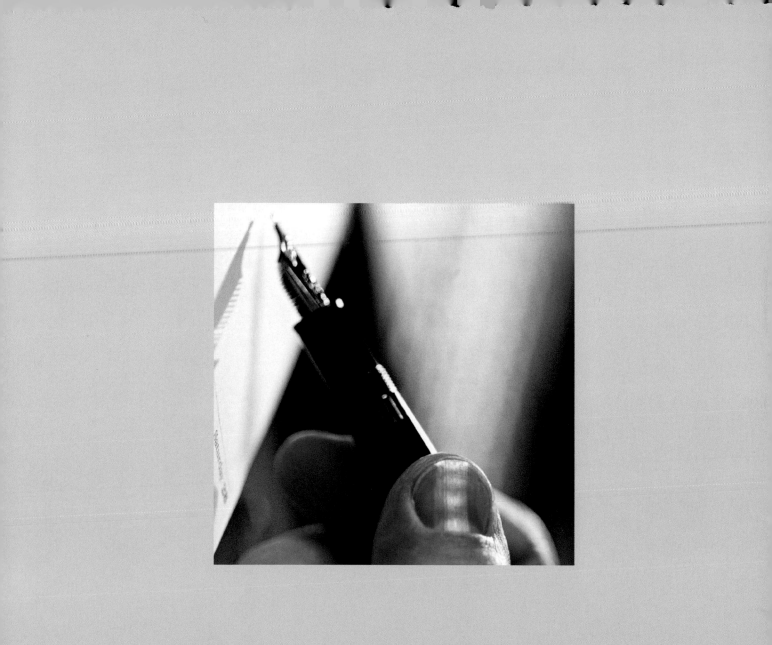

Natasha needs to do her homework.

She works on her **numbers**. **N**atasha

writes the **numbers** in her **n**otebook.

Natasha needs to clean her room.

She puts her **note**, her **notebook**, and

her **newspaper** into her backpack.

Natasha notices a **nickel** under her bed!

How many pennies equal a **nickel**?

It is nearly time for **N**atasha to go to

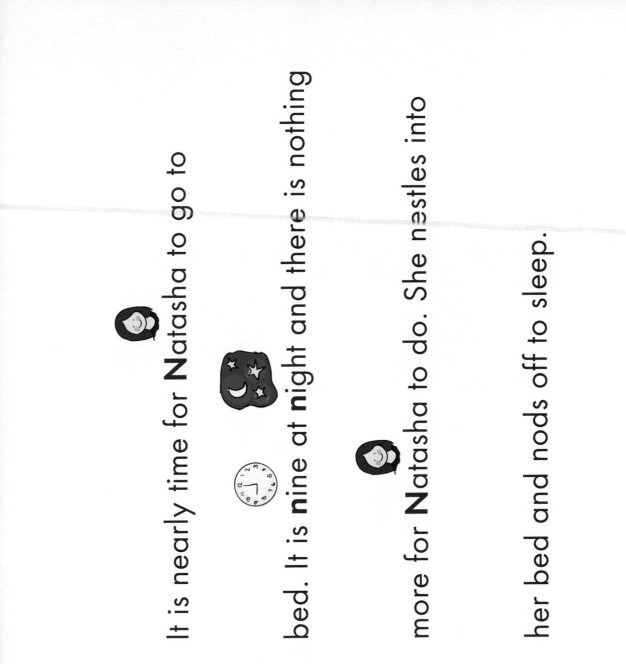

bed. It is **n**ine at **n**ight and there is nothing

more for **N**atasha to do. She nestles into

her bed and nods off to sleep.

Fun Facts

Newspapers are filled with information. Some newspapers focus on international news–stories about events all around the world. Other newspapers focus on national or local news, business, or the arts. Not all newspapers are printed on paper. You can read many newspapers on the Internet.

Did you figure out how many pennies equal a nickel? If you said a nickel is worth five pennies, you were right! The nickel is a U.S. coin made up of two kinds of metal–nickel and copper. The front of the coin shows Thomas Jefferson, the third president of the United States. The other side shows Jefferson's home, called Monticello.

People have been using numbers for thousands and thousands of years. Many different cultures throughout history developed their own way to write numbers. Today, most of the world uses the Arabic number system. In this system, all numbers can be written using just zero and the numerals 1 through 9.

To Read More

About the Letter N

Klingel, Cynthia. *Naps: The Sound of N.* Chanhassen, Minn.: The Child's World, 2000.

About Newspapers

Gibbons, Gail. *Deadline: From News to Newspaper.* New York: Crowell, 1987.

Leedy, Loreen. *The Furry News: How to Make a Newspaper.* New York: Holiday House, 1990.

About Nickels

Morrison, Taylor. *The Buffalo Nickel.* Boston: Houghton Mifflin, 2002.

Smalls-Hector, Irene, and Tyrone Geter (illustrator). *Irene and the Big Fine Nickel.* Boston: Houghton Mifflin, 2002.

About Numbers

Inkpen, Mick. *Kipper's Book of Numbers.* San Diego: Harcourt, 1999.

Stoddart, Matthew. *Fun with 1, 2, 3.* New York: Random House, 2000.

Words with N

Words with N at the Beginning

Natasha
nearly
needs
nestles
never
newspaper
nickel
night
nighttime
nine
nods
noon
note
notebook
nothing
notices
now
numbers

Words with N in the Middle

and
banana
beginning
end
enough
information
inside
into
many
nine
nothing
pennies
things
under

Words with N at the End

can
clean
horn
in
information
learn
noon
on

About the Authors

Cynthia Klingel has worked as a high school English teacher and an elementary teacher. She is currently the curriculum director for a Minnesota school district. Cynthia Klingel lives with her family in Mankato, Minnesota.

Robert B. Noyed started his career as a newspaper reporter. Since then, he has worked in communications and public relations for a Minnesota school district for more than fourteen years. Robert B. Noyed lives with his family in Brooklyn Center, Minnesota.